My Secret Unicorn

Snowy Dreams

Twilight's magic was fading! Lauren
couldn't believe it. No more magic. No
more flying. And maybe soon, no more
talking to her best friend.

But the worst thing of all was how
unhappy this was making Twilight. Did he
really think she wouldn't love him
anymore, just because he wasn't a
unicorn?

My Secret Unicorn

Snowy Dreams

Linda Chapman

Illustrated by Ann Kronheimer

Cover Illustration by Andrew Farley

SCHOLASTIC INC.

New York   Toronto   London   Auckland   Sydney
Mexico City   New Delhi   Hong Kong   Buenos Aires

ISBN-13: 978-0-545-03159-2

ISBN-10: 0-545-03159-1

12 11 10 9 8 7 6 5 4   7 8 9 10 11 12/0

Printed in the U.S.A.   40

First Scholastic printing, November 2007

To Jessica Duxbury, a very special friend

PROLOGUE

In a distant land, three Unicorn Elders stood beside a stone table. Their silvery manes swept to the floor and their snow-white coats gleamed in the moonlight. One had a golden horn, one had a silver, and the third had a bronze.

"It is time for us to find out," the silver-horned unicorn said softly.

The other two unicorns nodded their noble heads.

The first unicorn touched the tabletop with her silver horn. Purple smoke began to drift across the surface and the stone shone like a mirror. An image appeared. It showed a small gray pony grazing in a field near a farmhouse at nighttime. Behind the farm, almost hidden in shadow, rose the Blue Ridge Mountains of Virginia.

"It's Twilight," the bronze-horned unicorn said slowly.

The three unicorns exchanged looks.

"I am surprised," remarked the unicorn with the golden horn. "Twilight is very young." His voice sounded troubled.

The bronze-horned unicorn nodded.

"He is, and he has not been with his unicorn friend for long. But they have done many good things together — more than some unicorns and their friends do in many years."

"That is true." The unicorn with the golden horn looked at the others. "I wonder how Twilight will take the news."

"It is never easy," the silver-horned unicorn said quietly. Her dark eyes, shimmering like deep pools, watched Twilight for a moment. "I will go and tell him."

"When will you go, Sidra?" the other unicorns asked.

Sidra lifted her head, her horn glittering in the moonlight. "Tonight."

CHAPTER

One

Beep-beep-beep! Lauren Foster rubbed her eyes. Her alarm clock went off again. *Beep-beep-beep!* Fumbling at the side of her bed, she pressed the off switch on the clock, then sank back against her pillows. *What day is it?* she wondered sleepily.

Saturday! And not just any old Saturday, but the first day of Christmas vacation!

Lauren suddenly felt wide awake. She didn't have to go to school for over two whole weeks and she could spend every day with Twilight!

Jumping out of bed, she padded over to the window. Pulling the curtains open, she saw Twilight standing by his paddock gate and she smiled. The day she had gotten Twilight had been the best day of her life. *Well, almost,* she thought, remembering the time a few weeks after that when she had found out that Twilight wasn't just an ordinary pony — he was a secret unicorn! Now, when Lauren's parents and little brother, Max, were sleeping, she turned Twilight into his magical unicorn shape so that they could go flying and do good deeds using his magical powers. Lauren knew she was really lucky to have a pony, and she was even luckier to have a unicorn, too!

Twilight began to walk along the fence. Reaching the end of the field, he turned and paced back again. Lauren frowned. It wasn't like Twilight to be so restless. He usually waited patiently by the gate. *He must be hungry,* she decided.

Turning from the window, she pulled on her jeans and warm sweatshirt. As she got dressed, she planned the morning in her head. She'd feed Twilight his breakfast and then groom him. At nine-thirty, Mel and Jessica, her two best friends, were coming over on their ponies to go for a ride in the woods. The weekend before, the three of them had discovered a large clearing in the trees with banks and steep slopes. They'd had great fun riding there and had decided to go back again.

Today's going to be great! Lauren thought. Tying her long fair hair back in a ponytail, she hurried downstairs.

The rest of the house was quiet. Her dad's boots weren't on the porch so Lauren guessed he was out working on the family's farm. Buddy, Max's young Bernese mountain dog, jumped up when he saw her. She stopped to scratch his ears. "Max will be up soon," she told him.

Buddy wagged his tail and licked her hand. Grabbing an apple from the bowl, Lauren ran out of the house and down the frosty path to Twilight's field.

"Twilight!" she called.

Twilight stopped walking and looked around.

"Hi, boy!"

Whinnying, Twilight trotted to the gate. When he reached it, he pushed

his head against her, almost knocking her over.

"Steady!" Lauren laughed. "Yes, the apple's for you. Here you go."

But to her surprise, Twilight ignored the apple. Instead, he whickered and touched her hair and then her face with his muzzle.

"Are you OK?" Lauren asked.

Twilight stood still.

"Twilight?" Lauren said, feeling alarmed. "Is something the matter?"

To her relief, Twilight shook his head.

He could understand Lauren when he was a pony and talk back to her in his own way, but now Lauren wished he could speak to her properly, with words, like he did when he was a unicorn. She wanted to find out why he seemed so uneasy. "Are you feeling upset because I didn't come to see you last night?" she asked. "I'm sorry, but Mom and Dad had friends over for supper and I fell asleep before they went to bed. We can go flying tonight, I promise."

But her words didn't seem to make Twilight any happier. He nudged her with his muzzle again. Lauren frowned. He was OK, wasn't he?

Of course he is, she thought. She'd asked him if there was anything wrong and he'd said no. Pushing her concerns away, she stroked his tangled mane. Time to get a move on. He needed a good grooming before Jessica and Mel arrived!

✷ ✷ ✷

By half past nine, Twilight's gray coat was
spotless, his long tail and mane were brushed
out, and his hooves were shining with hoof
oil. But he still seemed restless, and Lauren
couldn't shake off the feeling that there was
something bothering him.

She had just finished tacking him up

when Mel and Jessica rode down the path on Shadow and Sandy.

Lauren waved. "Hi!"

"Twilight looks clean," Jessica commented.

"Pity about you, Lauren!" Mel grinned.

Lauren looked down at her clothes, which were very dusty after brushing Twilight, and grinned back. "Never mind. Twilight's the one that matters!"

The three ponies touched noses to say hello. They were almost as good friends as Mel, Jessica, and Lauren were. Lauren took hold of the reins and swung herself into the saddle. "Let's go!"

They rode down the path into the woods.

It was a bright cold morning and the winter sun shone through the treetops, melting the frost on the ground. As soon as the track widened out, the ponies began to pull at their bits.

"I think Sandy wants to canter," Jessica said, patting the young palomino pony's neck.

"What are you waiting for?" Mel shortened Sandy's reins as Shadow tossed his gray head. "Come on!"

Eventually they reached the clearing. It was a hilly area with lots of bushes and twisty paths leading up and down banks and steep slopes. At first, Lauren, Mel, and Jessica rode cautiously, but they soon grew in confidence and began to try the banks at a trot and a canter.

"What about that hill?" Mel suggested, pointing to a high bank that none of them had ridden down yet.

"No way," Jessica said. "It's much too steep."

Lauren was standing a little way off with Twilight. "What do you think, Twilight?" Twilight was startled when he heard his name and Lauren had the feeling she'd interrupted his thoughts. "Should we go down it?"

Twilight shook his head. "We're not going to do it, either," Lauren called to the others.

"I've got an idea!" Mel said. "Let's set a course over the rest of the clearing and then we can time ourselves and see who's the fastest."

It was great fun but Twilight didn't seem to be as lively as usual. He stumbled several times and once or twice Lauren had to press him on, when normally she had to try and slow him down.

"Are you sure you're all right, Twilight?" she whispered, reining him in.

Twilight nodded but Lauren wasn't convinced. *I'll ask him what's wrong when I turn him into a unicorn tonight,* she decided. *We'll be able to talk normally then.*

CHAPTER

Two

As soon as her parents went to bed that evening, Lauren slipped out of the house. The night air was freezing on her skin and the farm was quiet. Excitement surged through her as she ran down the dark path. Soon she and Twilight would be flying. She could almost feel the wind whipping through her hair, feel the warmth of Twilight's smooth back. What would they do tonight? Maybe they'd go to the woods and see what animals were around, or maybe jump over the treetops . . .

If Twilight's feeling OK, she reminded herself, thinking how oddly he'd been behaving that day.

"Twilight!" she called softly.

He whinnied.

Lauren reached the gate and quickly spoke the words of the Turning Spell.

> *"Twilight Star, Twilight Star,*
> *Twinkling high above so far.*
> *Shining light, shining bright,*
> *Will you grant my wish tonight?*
> *Let my little horse forlorn*
> *Be at last a unicorn!"*

There was a flash of purple light and Twilight was transformed from a pony into a unicorn. His gray coat gleamed snow-white, his mane and tail hung in silky strands and in the center of his forehead was a sparkling silver horn.

He stepped forward. "Hello, Lauren."

His mouth didn't move but Lauren could hear his voice clearly in her head so long as she was touching him or holding a hair from his mane. Nowadays, she made sure that she had one of his hairs with her at all times in case she needed to turn him into a unicorn and speak to him. "Are you all right?" she asked, stroking his forelock.

"I'm fine," Twilight said, but he let out a long sigh.

Lauren wondered why he seemed so

down. *Maybe if we go flying it will cheer him up.* "Do you want to go flying?" she suggested.

Twilight shook his head. "No. I don't feel like it."

Lauren was astonished. "Why not?" The only time she'd ever known Twilight to turn down the chance to go flying had been when he had been sick.

"I feel really tired after all the cantering and jumping today," Twilight replied.

"OK," Lauren said slowly. "I suppose we can always go tomorrow instead." She put her arms around his neck, feeling confused. It was not like Twilight to refuse a chance to go flying.

Another long, sad sigh trembled through him.

"Twilight, what is it?" Lauren asked, stepping back and looking at him. "Something's wrong, I know it is. Are you sick? Maybe I should get the vet?"

"No," Twilight said. "I don't feel sick. I'm . . . tired." He saw her concerned expression. "I really don't feel sick. I'd tell you if I did, I promise. I think I just need to rest. Will you turn me back into a pony, please?"

Lauren stroked him worriedly. Twilight wasn't behaving like himself at all. But what could she do? "OK," she said and, giving him a kiss, she said the Undoing Spell.

"Good night," she murmured as the purple flash faded and Twilight looked like an ordinary pony once again.

Twilight whickered softly, and Lauren headed back toward the house, hoping he'd feel better in the morning.

Lauren got up early the next day to check on Twilight. To her relief he whinnied cheerfully when he saw her.

"Are you feeling better?" she asked.

Twilight nodded.

He definitely seemed livelier. He was holding his head high and his eyes had lost their worried look. Lauren felt relieved. Perhaps he *had* just been tired the night before.

"We can go out for a ride later," she told him.

After they had both had breakfast and Lauren had groomed Twilight, she tacked him up and rode into the woods. She decided to ride to the clearing with the banks and hills again. It was different riding there on her own, instead of with Mel and Jessica, but Lauren didn't mind. It was another crisp, cold morning and it was great to be with Twilight, trotting along the frosty tracks. Everything was quiet, still, and peaceful.

When they reached the clearing, Lauren saw that there were two other riders already there. The girls looked a few years older than her — maybe twelve or thirteen. They were cantering down the banks on their ponies, shouting to each other. Lauren halted, not sure if she should join in.

"Perhaps we should go back," she murmured to Twilight. But then one of the girls' horses — a pretty bay Arab with four white socks — noticed them. She lifted her head and whinnied. Both girls looked around.

"Hi there!" called the girl on the bay mare. She had blonde hair tied in a short, stubby ponytail under her riding hat.

"Hi," Lauren said shyly.

"Were you coming to ride here?" the girl asked, riding over.

Lauren nodded. "But it doesn't matter. I can come back another day."

"No, it's OK," the girl said. "We don't mind. There's room for all of us. My name's Jo-Ann, by the way. And this is my pony, Beauty."

Lauren looked at the pretty bay mare with her dished face and large dark eyes. "She is beautiful."

"Thanks," Jo-Ann smiled. "So, what's your name?"

"Lauren. And this is Twilight."

The other girl came over. "I'm Grace," she said. "And this is Windfall," she added, patting the neck of her chestnut pony.

"Do you want to ride with us?" asked Jo-Ann.

"OK," Lauren agreed. She and Twilight set off after the others. He was smaller than the other two ponies but he kept up well, twisting and turning and cantering sure-footedly down the banks. Jo-Ann was a very daring rider. After cantering up and down the hills, she started to jump any bush or fallen log she could find — even logs that had spiky branches sticking up and that were lying on uneven ground. She didn't seem to worry about safety. Lauren and Grace stopped to watch her.

Lauren gasped as Beauty only just managed to clear a huge tree trunk.

"That was close!" Jo-Ann grinned, pulling Beauty up and patting her. She looked around. "What shall I do next?" Her eyes fell on the very steep bank. "I know! How about I try that bank over there?"

"No way!" Grace said. "It's much too steep and it might be slippery."

"I bet Beauty could manage it," Jo-Ann said thoughtfully.

"Don't do it," Grace advised. "These guys have done enough." She patted Windfall's warm neck. "Come on, let's take them home."

"I guess they are quite hot," Jo-Ann agreed reluctantly. "Let's walk back to cool them off." She turned to Lauren. "Nice to meet you, Lauren. See you around."

"Yeah, bye!" Lauren called.

She waved as the older girls rode off, and then stroked Twilight's mane. "Come on, let's go home, too." She didn't want to tire him out again. She was looking forward to flying that night!

As they reached the farm, Lauren saw Max and Buddy heading out along the drive. Max had his skateboard with him. "Are you going over to Leo and Steven's?" she asked.

Max nodded. "Yeah, Leo's got a new skateboard and he said I could try it, then we're going to take Buddy for a walk."

Buddy wagged his bushy tail and woofed. He might not be able to understand humans in the way that Twilight could, but he could certainly understand the words *Buddy* and *walk*!

"You'll like that, won't you, boy?" Max said, giving Buddy a hug. "You like Leo and Steven." Buddy licked his face in reply and Max giggled.

Lauren grinned. It was great seeing Max and Buddy so happy together. When Max had first made friends with their neighbors, Steven and Leo Vance, he had neglected Buddy a little bit, but then he had found out his new friends liked dogs as much as he did and now Buddy always went with him when he went to their house.

"See you later, Lauren," Max said, setting off again.

"Later," Lauren replied, and she rode Twilight back to his stable.

After she had untacked him and washed him down, she turned him out into the field. "I'll come out this evening and we can go flying. OK?"

Twilight didn't respond.

"Twilight?" Lauren said.

He whickered quietly. *Tonight,* Lauren thought, giving him a hug, and she went in for lunch.

⋆   ⋆   ⋆

That night, Twilight was waiting for Lauren by the gate. He seemed tense again; he was pacing up and down and his head was held high. Lauren quickly turned him into a unicorn. "Hi, boy. Are you ready to go flying?"

Twilight shook his head.

"Why not?" Lauren demanded. "We didn't do that much today!"

Twilight interrupted her. "It's not because I'm tired."

"So, why can't we go flying then?"

Twilight pawed the ground unhappily. "Because . . . because I can't."

Lauren didn't understand. "What do you mean, you can't?" She touched his neck in concern. "Are you sick or something?"

"No. I can't go flying because . . ." Twilight took a deep breath and looked miserably at her. "Because my magic powers have stopped working!"

CHAPTER

Three

Lauren stared. "What do you mean, your powers have stopped working? For how long?"

Twilight looked at the ground. "Forever."

Lauren felt as if a bucket of ice had just been poured all over her. "Forever." she echoed.

Twilight nodded. "It does happen sometimes," he said, not meeting her eyes. "Unicorns lose their powers. Their magic just fades and goes away. It means I can't do any magic anymore — I can't look into the seeing stones, I can't heal wounds, I can't make people feel braver. I can't do any of those things."

Lauren's mind seemed to spin. "And you can't fly?"

"No."

Lauren was struck by an awful thought. "But you'll always be able to turn into a unicorn, won't you? I'll always be able to speak to you like this?"

"I don't know." Twilight hesitated.

"Probably not," he added in a very small voice. "My powers will probably all disappear in the end."

Lauren's stomach plunged. She didn't know what to say.

"I . . . I suppose this means you won't love me anymore," Twilight said.

"What?" Lauren frowned. "Of course I'll love you."

Twilight looked taken aback. "But . . . but I won't be able to do magic. I'll just be an ordinary pony."

"As if that matters!" Lauren burst out. She was astonished that he could think this would change the way she felt about him. "Twilight, you're my best friend." She hugged him fiercely. "How *could* you think that losing your powers would change that? I loved you before I knew you were a unicorn, remember? It doesn't matter to me whether you're magical or not."

"So, you won't want me to go away?" Twilight spoke very slowly. "You won't want to get rid of me?"

"Get rid of you? No way!"

A look of confusion crossed Twilight's

face. "But . . . but I thought . . ." He looked even more upset than before.

"I can't believe you'd think that I'd want to get rid of you!" Lauren exclaimed. "All that matters, Twilight, is that we're together."

Twilight scraped his hoof on the ground. "Oh," he said in a very small voice.

Feeling utterly bewildered, Lauren put her arms around him. What was going on? A hard lump of tears blocked her throat. But she tried not to cry. Twilight was obviously very upset. She'd only make him more miserable if she started crying.

"Maybe I'd better turn you back into a pony," she said, her voice coming out in a whisper.

Twilight nodded sadly.

Lauren said the words of the Undoing
Spell and Twilight turned back into a
pony.

"'Night, Twilight," she whispered.

He whickered unhappily as she walked
slowly back to the house.

When she got back to her bedroom, she
sat down on the bed. Twilight's magic was
fading! She undressed and got into bed. She
couldn't believe it. No more magic. No
more flying. And, maybe soon, no more
talking to her best friend. But the worst
thing of all was how unhappy this was
making Twilight. Did he really think she
wouldn't love him anymore, just because
he wasn't a unicorn?

* * *

Lauren lay awake for ages that night and when she woke up, her first thought was that she'd had a bad dream. She blinked, and realized it hadn't been a dream at all. It was real. Twilight was losing his magic powers.

She pulled on her clothes and went downstairs. Her mom, dad, and Max were in the kitchen.

"Morning, sleepyhead!" her dad teased.

Not wanting her parents to see how tired she felt in case they wanted to know why, Lauren forced a smile. "Morning."

Mrs. Foster was making a pot of coffee. "We almost sent Buddy in to wake you up.

Twilight will be wondering where his breakfast is."

"I'll go and feed him now," Lauren said, glad of an excuse to get out of the house.

Buddy trotted over to her and pushed his body between her legs. Lauren made a fuss over him to try and hide her sadness from her family. When she sat down to pull her boots on, Buddy plonked his head on her lap and looked up at her with big brown eyes. It was as if he could sense there was something wrong.

"Good boy," Lauren whispered, blinking hard.

"What time are you going over to Leo and Steven's, Max?" Mrs. Foster asked.

Max scraped the last of his cereal bowl clean. "Half past nine. I can't wait! They got their new puppy last night."

Lauren had forgotten that Steven and Leo were getting their new puppy that weekend.

"Have they decided what they're going to call her?" asked Mrs. Foster.

Max grinned. "Buggy!"

"Buggy?" Mrs. Foster echoed doubtfully.

"It's short for Love Bug. That's what Steven and Leo's mom said the puppy's full name is."

Mr. Foster shook his head. "Buddy and Buggy. That's going to be a bit confusing!"

"I think Buggy's a cool name. She and Buddy are going to be best friends!" Max said happily. "I can't wait to see her."

Mrs. Foster smiled. "I'm with you there. In fact, I think I might just have to walk over with you when you go to their house this morning." She glanced at Lauren. "Do you want to come too, Lauren?"

Knowing that her mom would think it was strange if she said no, Lauren nodded. "Yes, please." She stood up and went to the door. First she had to feed Twilight. As she walked down to his field, she felt odd. She wasn't quite sure how to act. What would she say to him?

Twilight was standing by the gate looking very miserable. His head was low and his eyes seemed to have lost their sparkle.

"Hey, boy," Lauren said.

He nuzzled her gently. Neither of them met the other's eyes.

Lauren fetched Twilight his breakfast, but he hardly touched it. He nibbled a few flakes of the coarse mix and then left the rest.

Lauren stroked him. "Not feeling hungry today?"

Twilight shook his head.

"Me neither," Lauren told him. Just

looking at how sad Twilight was made her eyes prickle with tears.

But he'll still be my pony, she reminded herself. *I'll still be able to see him and ride him every day. And the more fuss I make over him, the more he might believe that I do still love him.*

Feeling a little bit better, she started on the stable chores — cleaning out and refilling Twilight's water buckets, brushing the concrete in front of the stables, and tidying the tack room. After a while, she heard her mom calling.

"Lauren! We're going to Steven and Leo's now!"

"Coming!" Lauren called back.

She went over to where Twilight was standing unhappily by the gate and rubbed his neck. "I'll be back soon," she promised, giving him a kiss.

Buggy was the cutest puppy ever! She was a flat-coated retriever with a soft, jet-black coat, bright sparkling eyes, big paws, and a tail that never seemed to stop wagging. As Lauren and Max and Mrs. Foster crowded around, the puppy wriggled in Leo's arms, trying to lick everyone's faces and hands with her pink tongue. Buddy pressed forward and Buggy licked him on the nose.

"Can I put her on the grass, Mom?" Leo begged.

"Yeah," Steven said. "Let's see how she likes Buddy."

Their mom, Helen, nodded. "All right."

As soon as Buggy was on the ground, she bounded over to Buddy, her tail going round and round like a propeller. She was only as high as his tummy, but she didn't seem scared at all. She leapt on Buddy, licking his mouth and pulling at his ears.

Buddy's tail started to wag, and he crouched down to look at her more closely.

The puppy yapped at him, and he woofed back in a deep voice. Then he lay down and let her jump all over him, rolling over on his back so she could climb onto his tummy.

After a few minutes they jumped up and began to chase each other around the garden.

"Looks like they're going to be friends," Helen smiled.

Leo turned to Max. "When Buggy gets bigger we'll be able to take them on walks together."

"And she can run around the skateboard course like Buddy does," said Steven.

"We can have races!" Leo added.

Max nodded eagerly. "It'll be cool!"

Lauren smiled. Max was going to have loads of fun taking Buddy to play with Leo, Steven, and Buggy. She knew that having friends with pets was great fun. She loved riding with Mel and Jessica.

And I'll still be able to do that when Twilight's magic is gone, she reflected. She thought of

Twilight's sad face that morning and suddenly wanted to get back to him. She had to make him realize that it didn't matter if he lost his magic.

"Is it OK if I go back now, Mom?" she asked.

"Of course," replied Mrs. Foster. "I'll see you later."

Lauren hurried home. Twilight was standing by the gate where she had left him, not looking any happier. Climbing over it, Lauren put an arm around his neck and leaned her cheek against his neck. "Oh, Twilight," she whispered. "Losing your powers must be horrible for you but it's going to be OK, I promise. We'll still be able to have lots of fun together."

She'd hoped her words might cheer Twilight up, but he still looked miserable.

Lauren wracked her brains to think of something she could do to make him feel better. Maybe if they went out for a ride in the woods it would help him realize how much fun they could have, even if he was just a pony.

"How about we go for a ride?" she suggested. "We could go to the place with the banks and hills again."

Twilight gave a tiny nod.

Lauren kissed him. "OK. I'll go and call Mel and Jessica and see if they want to come too."

CHAPTER

Four

Jessica couldn't come out for a ride because she was going into town with her stepsister, Samantha, but Mel was excited to go to the woods again.

She came over at eleven. "So, did you go to the clearing yesterday?" she asked as they rode down the track, away from the farm.

"Yes," Lauren replied. "There were two

girls there. They let me ride with them."
She patted Twilight. "We had fun, didn't
we, boy?" He snorted quietly. Lauren
crossed her fingers. She desperately wanted
him to see what a good time they could
have without magic.

As they reached the clearing they heard
voices.

"That might be those girls," Lauren said.

She and Mel rode into the clearing. Sure
enough, Jo-Ann and Grace were
there on Beauty and Windfall. They had set
up jumps at the bottom of some of
the banks.

"Hi, Lauren!" Jo-Ann called, waving. She
looked again. "Mel!" she exclaimed. "Hello."

"Hi, Jo-Ann," Mel called.

"Do you two know each other?" Lauren asked in surprise.

Mel nodded as Jo-Ann rode over to them. "Our moms are friends," she explained. She smiled at Jo-Ann. "Is this your new pony? Mom told me you'd just got one."

"Yes, this is Beauty," Jo-Ann replied. The pretty bay tossed her head. "She's beautiful. She's really fast and loves jumping. Is Shadow still jumping OK?"

Mel nodded. "Ever since last summer he's been fine."

Lauren stroked Twilight's neck to hide a smile. When she had first met Mel, Shadow had been scared of jumping, but she and Twilight had helped him get over his fear. It had been one of the first things they had done together after Lauren had found out Twilight was a unicorn. He had been able to use his magic powers to fill Shadow with courage — enough to leap out of his barn when it was on fire! She wondered if he was remembering it too.

I suppose we won't be helping any more people now. Lauren pushed the thought away. This wasn't the time to feel sorry for herself. Twilight needed her to be cheerful.

"Can we try the jumps?" she asked Jo-Ann.

"Sure," Jo-Ann replied.

"Come on!" Grace called.

Soon, Lauren and Mel were cantering down the banks and over the jumps with the two older girls. Mel only did the lower jumps but Lauren tried some of the bigger ones. Not all of them, though. Jo-Ann had made a few huge jumps out of logs and old branches.

"I don't know how you dare do that!" Mel called as Jo-Ann rode down a particularly steep bank with a huge brush jump at the bottom.

"It's fun!" Jo-Ann laughed, pulling Beauty to a halt. The pony snorted and pulled at her bit.

"Why don't you try it?" Jo-Ann urged Lauren and Mel.

Mel shook her head. "It's way too big for Shadow and me."

Jo-Ann turned to Lauren. "How about you, Lauren? Twilight seems really good at jumping."

Lauren hesitated. Part of her longed to canter down the bank and fly over the jump, but then she looked at the steep uneven surface and shook her head. Jo-Ann might have managed it fine but it did look tricky. She'd never forgive herself if Twilight got hurt. "No, I don't think I will," she said.

Jo-Ann looked teasingly at her. "Chicken!"

"Jo-Ann!" Grace protested. "Don't hassle Lauren. If she doesn't want to do it, she doesn't have to."

"Sorry." Jo-Ann shrugged. "Looks like

I'll have to do it on my own, then." She cantered toward the bank and sped down it. Beauty cleared the jump easily.

Jo-Ann patted her and headed toward the really steep bank that no one had dared to go down yet.

"Be careful, Jo!" Grace warned.

"Stop fussing," Jo-Ann replied. "Beauty will manage it fine."

The other three watched as she headed toward it. Beauty sped up, fighting for her head. Jo-Ann circled her, got her steady, and then tried again. It was so steep that Beauty had to tuck her hocks right underneath her. Lauren gasped as the bank crumbled a little and Beauty slid a few feet, but Jo-Ann sat very still and let her find her footing again. In a couple more strides, they safely reached the bottom of the bank.

"Good girl!" Jo-Ann praised.

"Cool!" Mel said.

Grace nodded. "That was great riding, Jo."

"She's a great pony!" Jo-Ann said, patting the mare. She looked at the bank. "Maybe I could put a jump at the bottom."

Grace shook her head. "It's hard enough to get down without a jump there."

"I suppose," Jo-Ann replied, not sounding convinced.

"Come on," Grace said. "Why don't we take the ponies to the creek for a drink?"

"All right." Jo-Ann turned to Lauren and Mel. "Are you going to come, too?"

They nodded and the four of them set off through the trees. As they rode, Lauren learned that Grace and Jo-Ann kept their ponies at a livery stable that Grace's mom owned. It was fun hearing about the ponies there, and about all the shows that Grace and Jo-Ann competed in. Lauren hoped Twilight was enjoying himself too.

It doesn't matter one bit that he can't be a unicorn, she told herself. *We'll still be able to go for rides like this and do all sorts of things.*

After all, Mel and Jessica love Shadow and Sandy and they aren't unicorns.

Lauren frowned as she realized she'd been so shocked by the news the night before that she hadn't asked Twilight why unicorns lost their powers at all, or if there was any way of stopping it. Perhaps there was some way of getting his powers back! Hope flickered through her. If there was anything — anything at all — she could do, then she would give it a try to make him happy again.

I'll ask him tonight, she thought. Then another idea struck her. What about her unicorn book? It had lots of information about unicorns in it. Maybe one of the chapters would explain how they could stop Twilight's magic from fading.

I'll look at it when I get home, she decided.

As soon as Lauren untacked Twilight after their ride, she ran into the house and found her precious book. *The Life of a Unicorn* was a very old book with a faded blue cover. Mrs. Fontana, who owned the bookshop in town, had given it to Lauren when she had first got Twilight. Mrs. Fontana was one of the few people who knew about Twilight, because she had once owned a unicorn herself.

Lauren began to leaf through the yellowing pages. There were chapters on unicorn myths, unicorn habits, and all sorts of information about Arcadia, the magic land that the unicorns came from.

Lauren flicked through chapter after chapter. There had to be something about unicorns losing their powers!

She stopped at the end of the book. There was nothing. Not a single mention of a unicorn's magic fading.

Weird, Lauren thought. *Twilight made it sound like it happened quite often. It's odd the book doesn't say anything about it at all.*

She frowned. She'd have to question him more that night.

"Twilight, I looked in the unicorn book and it didn't say anything about unicorns losing their powers," Lauren said. She had just turned Twilight into a unicorn.

"Well, it does happen," Twilight said quickly.

"Is there anything that can be done to stop it or to bring them back?" Lauren asked.

"No," he muttered, scraping at the ground with his front hoof. "I don't think so."

"Maybe if you tell me everything you know about it, we can think of something to try," Lauren urged him.

Twilight looked uncomfortable. "I can't remember much."

Lauren frowned. "How can we find out more?" Her eyes widened. "Of course!"

she exclaimed. "Mrs. Fontana! She knows lots about unicorns — we can ask her."

Twilight shook his head. "I'm sure she won't be able to help, Lauren . . ."

But Lauren refused to give up hope. "It's worth asking her," she interrupted. Mrs. Fontana always seemed to know what to do when there was a problem with Twilight. "I'll see if Mom will drive me to her shop in the morning." She hugged Twilight. "Don't worry, Mrs. Fontana will be able to help us, I'm sure!"

Twilight snorted unhappily. Lauren couldn't understand why he didn't look convinced. After all, if he was so depressed about losing his magic powers, surely he'd try anything to get them back?

CHAPTER

Five

Deep in the heart of Arcadia, the three Unicorn Elders stood by the stone table, their golden, silver, and bronze horns sparkling in the moonlight. The picture that had been there moments before had vanished and all that was left of the magic was a wisp of purple smoke drifting across the table.

"Twilight is very unhappy," Ira, the unicorn with the golden horn, said heavily.

"He is so young," sighed Rohan, the bronze-horned unicorn. "And he loves Lauren very much."

Sidra lifted her head, her silver horn flashing in the moonlight. "Yes, but this is how it has to be." She pricked up her ears. "He must see that this is for the best — that it is an honor to be chosen. Maybe I should visit him again and talk to him some more."

"Yes," the other two unicorns agreed.

"Will you go tomorrow night?" Ira asked.

Sidra nodded. "I will."

"Is there something in particular you want from the bookshop?" Mrs. Foster asked as she drove Lauren into town the next morning. It was a very cold day and the sky was turning a snowy white.

"I just want a new book to read," Lauren replied casually. "I've got the money that Aunt Hilary sent to me, and I thought I might spend it on a book."

Mrs. Foster nodded. "Any idea what book you'd like?"

"Not yet," Lauren said. "Is it OK if I spend some time browsing?"

"Well, it looks like it's going to snow, so we'd better not be too long," her mom replied. "I'll leave you at Mrs. Fontana's while I do the rest of my shopping."

"Thanks," Lauren said, feeling relieved. Hopefully she'd get to spend some time

with Mrs. Fontana on her own. She stared
out of the window at the houses flashing by
and, as soft snowflakes began to fall, she
wondered what Mrs. Fontana would say.

Mrs. Fontana's bookshop never seemed to
change. There were always piles of books on
the floor and the air always smelled slightly
of black currants. Lauren thought it was the
smell of magic even though her mom said

it was the fruit tea that Mrs. Fontana drank. The elderly lady was sitting by the fireplace with her gray hair tied back in a bun and her soft yellow shawl wrapped round her shoulders. She was talking to Walter, her little black-and-white terrier dog.

"Hello, Lauren," she said, looking up as Lauren entered. "How are you?"

"Fine, thank you," Lauren replied. She glanced around to check that there was no one else in the shop.

"We're alone," Mrs. Fontana said, as if she could read Lauren's thoughts. She frowned. "Are you all right, my dear? You look worried."

The words burst out of Lauren. "Oh, Mrs. Fontana, I really need your help. Twilight's losing his magic powers!"

Mrs. Fontana looked astonished. "What?"

Lauren quickly told her everything. "He said that it happens to unicorns sometimes but I can't find any mention of it in the book and I want to know if there's anything we can do. It's making him so unhappy!"

She looked pleadingly at Mrs. Fontana. "Do you know if there's anything that will stop his magic from fading?"

Mrs. Fontana looked puzzled. "I'm sorry, Lauren, but I don't know what to say. I've never heard of a unicorn losing its powers before — not permanently, anyway. Are you sure that's what Twilight said was happening?"

"Positive," Lauren replied. "He said it happens often and that there's nothing we can do."

"How strange." Mrs. Fontana rubbed her forehead. "Why don't you tell me exactly what happened?"

Lauren sat on a long-legged stool and rested her chin on her hands. "He was fine one day, and the next he seemed really miserable. At first he said he was just tired but then he told me about his magic fading. He's so unhappy! I've tried telling him that I'll still love him even if he's just a regular pony, but it doesn't seem to have helped." She bit her lip. "It's awful seeing him like this, Mrs. Fontana! If there's anything I can do, I want to do it."

"I'm sure you do, Lauren." Mrs. Fontana hesitated. "But you know, I think there's something else going on and Twilight's not telling you everything. Unicorns don't lose their powers permanently. It just doesn't happen."

Lauren's heart leaped. "Really?"

Mrs. Fontana nodded.

"So why have Twilight's powers gone away?" Lauren asked. "Why can't he fly anymore?"

"I don't know," Mrs. Fontana admitted. "I can only assume that there's something Twilight hasn't told you about. My advice is to try and get him to talk to you. But don't push him too hard," she warned. "He might clam up even more."

"OK," Lauren agreed. Her head was whirling. It felt odd to think that there was something Twilight wasn't telling her. "I just don't understand why he would keep something secret. I'm his best friend — he should be able to tell me anything!"

"Oh, Lauren, people keep secrets for all sorts of reasons," Mrs. Fontana replied.

"Twilight is probably doing what he thinks is best. Just let him know that you'll listen when he's ready to talk." She squeezed Lauren's hand. "He might be your unicorn, Lauren, but he's also your friend. Treat him like you would any of your other friends if you thought they had a problem. He'll tell you what's going on in his own good time."

Just then the doorbell tinkled and a man came in with a little boy. Walter trotted over to say hello, and Lauren knew her conversation with Mrs. Fontana was over.

"Thanks, Mrs. Fontana," she said.

"Good luck!" Mrs. Fontana smiled. "And now, you'd better choose a book before your mom gets back and wonders what you've been doing all this time."

Lauren thought about what Mrs. Fontana had said for the rest of the day. She felt better knowing that Mrs. Fontana had never heard of a unicorn's magic fading away permanently before. She just wished she knew exactly what was going on.

"Are you sure there's nothing else you want to tell me?" Lauren said to Twilight as she stroked his silky mane that night.

"No," he sighed.

"Really sure?" Lauren persisted.

"Yes. Let's talk about something else."

Lauren bit her lip with frustration. She

remembered what Mrs. Fontana had said about letting Twilight talk to her in his own time, so she just nodded. "Sure. But you can tell me anything, Twilight, you know that. Anything at all."

He stared miserably at the ground. Lauren couldn't bear seeing him look so sad.

"I know, how about I go and get you some carrots from the tack room as a treat? Dad put a new sack in there this afternoon."

Twilight nodded and she hurried away.

When she came back with the carrots, Twilight was shaking his head. "I've got to tell her!" he was muttering. "I can't do this."

Lauren froze. What was he talking about?"

"I just can't!" Twilight said to himself.

"Twilight?" Lauren whispered.

Twilight looked around, startled. "Lauren! I didn't see you there."

"What are you talking about?" she asked, hurrying over. "What have you got to tell me?"

"Nothing. I . . . I wasn't talking about you," Twilight said quickly.

Lauren felt her temper flare. She knew that wasn't true. "Twilight!" she exclaimed angrily. "Just . . ." She broke off, recalling what Mrs. Fontana had said about not putting pressure on him in case he clammed up even more. "OK," she said, trying to stay calm. "If you don't want to talk about it, that's fine."

Twilight relaxed slightly and as she fed him a carrot, she changed the subject. "It was fun yesterday, wasn't it? Riding with Jo-Ann and Grace, I mean. Do you like Beauty and Windfall?"

Twilight nodded. "Yes, and I liked cantering up and down the banks, too."

"We'll have to go again," Lauren said. "And go on some more fun rides and wander by the creek. There are so many things we can do, especially when summer comes," she went on, trying to remind him that they could have fun whether he was a unicorn or not. "Maybe we could even go camping!"

"Maybe," Twilight said in a quiet voice.

Lauren stayed with him for an hour,

talking about all the great things they could do together, before she went inside. She sat down on her bed, feeling frustrated. However nice it was talking to Twilight, she still hadn't found out what was going on.

Getting undressed, she climbed into bed and pulled her blanket over her. But she couldn't sleep. She and Twilight were best friends. They shouldn't keep secrets from each other. *I wouldn't keep a secret from him,* she thought.

She hesitated and then pushed her blanket back. She couldn't go on like this. Mrs. Fontana might have said to take it easy but she *had* to know what was going on.

Getting out of bed, she put her clothes back on. Then she crept downstairs and hurried outside. She would beg Twilight to tell her what was wrong, make him see that whatever it was, they could overcome it together.

Feeling fired up with determination, she ran down the path to his field. Suddenly she stopped.

"Twilight!" she whispered in astonishment.

Twilight was standing in his field, but he wasn't a pony, like she had left him. His coat was gleaming silvery-white and his horn was glittering. He was a unicorn!

And that wasn't all. Standing beside him was another unicorn! It had its head bent and was talking urgently to Twilight. Lauren stared in shock. This unicorn was bigger than Twilight, with a coat that sparkled like freshly fallen snow. It had a long silver horn, glittering dark eyes, and a face so beautiful that just looking at it made Lauren hold her breath.

The unicorn whinnied and flew into the air without noticing Lauren.

Stunned, Lauren watched Twilight plunge upward, too, and side by side the two unicorns cantered away into the starry sky.

CHAPTER

Six

Lauren took a step forward and stared at the empty sky. Twilight had said he couldn't fly any more. He had told her that his powers had gone. How *could* he have just flown away?

There was only one answer. Twilight had been lying to her!

Lauren shook her head in disbelief. She

couldn't believe that all this time, when she'd been so worried about him, he hadn't lost his powers at all.

Turning, she ran back to the house.

When she reached her bedroom, she threw herself down on her bed. The unicorn book slipped on to the floor and landed with a thud. It fell awkwardly, half open, with its beautiful old pages bent and creased. Lauren automatically reached down to pick it up. As she did, she noticed that it had fallen open at a picture. Icy fingers ran down her spine. It showed two unicorns cantering into the sky — one big, one small, exactly like Twilight and the unicorn she'd seen just now.

With her heart thudding painfully, Lauren pulled the book closer and read the title below the picture:

A Unicorn Elder taking a Chosen Unicorn back to Arcadia.

Not understanding, Lauren scanned the rest of the words.

Pony unicorns who prove themselves to be particularly brave and resourceful in the human world will often be chosen to return to Arcadia. There they will train to be assistants to the Unicorn Elders, helping the Elders to rule Arcadia and watch over the human world. It is a great honor to be chosen and, in time, these chosen unicorns will one day become Unicorn Elders themselves. A chosen unicorn will be visited by a Unicorn Elder several times before the unicorn has to say good-bye to his or her human friend and leave the human world forever.

Leave the human world forever. The words echoed around in Lauren's head. Twilight must have been chosen to go to Arcadia! Was that where he'd been going with the other unicorn tonight?

Did that mean she was never going to see him again?

Jumping off her bed, Lauren raced to her window.

Twilight was in his field, grazing peacefully. For one wild moment Lauren wondered if she'd just imagined the sight of him flying into the sky with another unicorn. Maybe it was all a dream? But it wasn't. She'd seen both unicorns flying away as clearly as she saw Twilight in his field now.

She sank down on to the window seat. The Unicorn Elder must have been visiting Twilight that night. But maybe the *next* time . . .

"No," Lauren whispered out loud. "He can't go to Arcadia."

But the more she thought about it, the more it all made sense. That first morning when he'd been so quiet — well, that must have been after the first visit from the Unicorn Elder, after Twilight had been told he'd been chosen. And the reason he had looked so sad even when Lauren had said she didn't mind if he lost his powers must have been because he'd known that they wouldn't be together much longer.

Why didn't he tell me? Lauren thought desperately. *He must have known he was going to have to tell me some time. Unless . . .*

Her stomach flipped over.

Perhaps Twilight hadn't been planning to tell her at all. Perhaps he'd been intending just to vanish one night.

Twilight wouldn't do that, she told herself, but why else would Twilight have kept his news as a secret? Why else would he have lied to her?

Lauren began to tremble. Moving like a robot, she took off her clothes and pulled on her pajamas, then crawled under the blanket. She couldn't stop shivering. She felt utterly betrayed by her best friend. How could he have thought of leaving without telling her? How could he have thought of leaving at all?

Oh, Twilight, she cried silently in her head. *I could never leave you.*

Pulling the blanket over her head, a sob choked through her and soon her pillow was soaked with tears.

* * *

The next morning, Lauren stayed in bed until she heard her mom getting up. For the first time ever, she didn't want to go out to Twilight's field. But when she heard her mom waking Max up, she knew she couldn't stay in bed much longer. She had to get up now to avoid facing her mom and Max in the kitchen. They would see at once that she'd been crying. Putting on her crumpled jeans, she hurried outside before they came downstairs.

Twilight was waiting by his gate. To Lauren's surprise, he lifted his head and whinnied happily. When she reached the gate he nuzzled her as if they were best friends again.

Her heart sank with misery. She knew why he was happy this morning. It was because he'd spent the night before talking to the other unicorn, and planning his return to Arcadia.

She pushed him away. "I'll get your breakfast," she said, barely able to stop her voice from shaking with hurt. Ignoring his look of surprise, she walked away.

When she returned with his coarse mix, Twilight whinnied.

"Here," she said abruptly, putting the bucket down.

Twilight nudged her but she stepped back. "No, don't do that!" she exclaimed.

Twilight took a mouthful and then, looking at her playfully from under his

forelock, he snorted the food into the air.
Normally when he messed around, it made
Lauren smile. But right then, her heart felt
like a stone in her chest. How could he be
so cheerful when he knew he was leaving
her forever?

She guessed that whatever the other
unicorn had said to him the night before

had made Twilight realize that his decision to leave was the right one.

Her throat ached. Turning around, she hurried away before he could see the tears in her eyes.

Twilight whickered, but she ignored him and carried on. She forced herself not to turn round even though he whinnied again and again. He was still whinnying when she reached the house and went inside, slamming the door behind her.

After breakfast, Lauren went to her room. To avoid going outside, she decided to tidy her room. She had just taken all the books off the shelves above her bed when Mel called.

"Hi!" Mel said cheerfully. "Do you want to go for a ride today? There isn't much snow — we could go to the clearing again."

"Um . . . no thanks." Lauren didn't feel like doing anything with Twilight.

"Why not?" Mel said in surprise.

"I don't feel very well," Lauren lied.

"What's the matter?" asked Mel.

Lauren thought quickly. "I've got a cold. My throat's really sore. I'd better not talk for long."

"Oh, OK. Well, I hope you feel better soon," Mel told her. "I'll give you a call tonight. Maybe we could go for a ride tomorrow?"

"Maybe," Lauren whispered. Saying good-bye, she put the phone down.

She walked over to the window and stared out. Twilight was standing by the gate with his ears pricked up hopefully. He looked like he was waiting for her. How could he not realize how much he was hurting her?

Wrapping her arms around herself, Lauren tried to imagine life without him. No unicorn, no pony, no best friend.

As if sensing that she was watching, Twilight looked up at the window. Swallowing her tears, Lauren quickly turned away.

CHAPTER

Seven

As Lauren fed Twilight that evening and refilled his water buckets, he nudged her again and again. Lauren guessed he was trying to tell her that he wanted to be turned into a unicorn.

"I'm not going to come out later," she muttered. "I'll see you in the morning, Twilight." *If you're still here.*

Twilight whickered urgently but Lauren shook her head.

Her heart aching, she trudged back to the house.

She was just pulling her boots off when the phone rang. It was Jessica. "Hi. How are you feeling?"

"Fine," Lauren said, before remembering she was supposed to be ill. "My throat's still a bit sore though," she added hastily.

"Mel said you weren't well. She's here now — she's staying the night."

"Hi, Lauren!" Lauren heard Mel shout in the background.

"Are you going to be OK to ride tomorrow?" Jessica asked.

"I'm not sure," Lauren said. "I don't think so."

"Is everything all right?" said Jessica. "You sound really down."

"I'm OK," Lauren told her.

Mel took the phone from Jessica. "Are you still feeling sick?"

"Yes." Lauren quickly changed the subject. "How was the ride today?"

"Fun," Mel answered. "We went to the clearing again after lunch. Jo-Ann and Grace weren't there this time."

Lauren could hear Twilight whinnying but she ignored him. "Jo-Ann had a riding lesson today and was going to go to the clearing later this afternoon," Lauren said.

"Yes, that's right," said Mel. "She must have gotten there after us. I wonder if she tried that bank again. She's so brave!"

"Yeah," Lauren said.

"Well, I'd better go," Mel told her. "I'll call you tomorrow. Get better soon! Jess and I want to go on as many rides as we can before it gets really snowy but we don't want to go without you."

Lauren hung up the phone and sat down. When Twilight left she wouldn't be able to go riding with Mel and Jessica any more. Slowly, her unhappiness turned to anger. *I'll get another pony,* she thought. *I don't need Twilight. I don't need him at all.*

She stood up and started setting the table for supper. Max was staying at Steven and Leo's house that night so it was just her and her mom and dad. She had just finished setting three places when the phone rang again.

Lauren picked it up. "Granger's Farm, Lauren Foster speaking."

"Oh hello, Lauren. It's Mrs. Cassidy."

"Hi," said Lauren, wondering why Mel's mom was calling her when Mel was staying at Jessica's house.

"Is your mom there?"

"Yes, I'll get her." Lauren called to her mom. "Mrs. Cassidy's on the phone!"

Her mom came into the kitchen and took the receiver. "Hi." Lauren was about to leave the room when she heard her mom's voice change. "Really?" Mrs. Foster sounded alarmed. "The pony came back on her own?"

Lauren frowned. *Pony? What pony?*

"Of course we'll help," her mom was saying. "I'll get Mike and we'll come right over."

"What was that about?" Lauren asked as her mom put the phone down.

"A friend of the Cassidys' went riding in the woods this afternoon, and her pony came back without her half an hour ago. The pony seems fine but the girl hasn't been seen since. Her mom's organizing a search party."

"What is the girl's name?" Lauren said, her heart beating faster.

"Jo-Ann," Mrs. Foster replied, heading out of the kitchen.

"Jo-Ann!" Lauren echoed.

"Do you know her?" Mrs. Foster asked.

"I've met her in the woods a few times." Lauren dug her nails into her palms. Jo-Ann was in trouble!

"Well, hopefully we'll find her soon," said Mrs. Foster, peering doubtfully through the window. It was already getting dark and it had started to snow again. "I'm going to get your dad and head over to the Cassidys' place. Do you want to come?"

Lauren hesitated, thinking fast. "No," she said. "I think I'll stay here."

"OK. I'll call you when there's some news." Mrs. Foster kissed her. "And try not to worry, honey. I'm sure we'll find Jo-Ann."

Lauren watched her mom getting into the truck and heading off to the barns. What should she do?

There was only one answer.

As soon as the truck's headlights disappeared down the drive, she pulled on her boots and coat and began to run down the path to Twilight's field.

"Twilight!" she shouted. "Twilight! Quick!"

CHAPTER

Eight

Twilight's whinny reached Lauren long before she could see him. As she raced up to the gate, heart pounding, he trotted over, whickering in delight.

She panted out the words of the Turning Spell. In a flash, Twilight turned into a unicorn.

"Lauren, what's the —"

"Listen," she interrupted him. "I've only turned you into a unicorn because I need your help. Jo-Ann's missing. I think she might have fallen off somewhere in the forest and we need to find her. I want you to use your magic to look into a seeing stone and see where she is."

Twilight started to speak. "But —"

"Don't tell me you can't do it!" Lauren burst out, her anger and hurt spilling over. "I *know* you can. I know you've just been lying to me because you don't want to be my unicorn anymore!"

Twilight was astounded. "What?"

"Just do the magic, Twilight!" Lauren exclaimed furiously. "Then you can go back to Arcadia! Yes, I know that's what you're planning," she went on. "I know you've been visited by a Unicorn Elder to talk about it, but right now I don't care." Tears burned in her eyes. "Just help Jo-Ann. Then you can go!"

"But Lauren!" Twilight protested. "I'm not going anywhere."

"Don't lie!" Lauren cried. "I know it's true."

"It's not!" Twilight insisted. "It's true a Unicorn Elder did come and ask me to go to Arcadia. She told me I'd been chosen to be an assistant to the Elders, but last night, I saw her again and told her I wouldn't go." His voice dropped. "I told her I couldn't leave you, Lauren."

Lauren stared at him. "You're . . . you're not going back?" she whispered.

Twilight shook his head. "The Unicorn Elder told me that if I don't go, I might lose my unicorn powers for real, but I don't care." He looked at Lauren with his dark eyes. "You're right. As long as we're together, nothing else matters. I'm your unicorn, Lauren, whether I can do magic or not."

Lauren swallowed. "You lied to me," she said in a shakey voice. "You told me your powers were going."

"I'm sorry," Twilight mumbled, looking wretched. "I only did it because I couldn't bear to hurt you. I thought that if I said my magic was fading, you wouldn't mind so much when I went away. But now I'm not going anywhere — I've said no!"

Lauren's mind whirled. *He wasn't going. It had all been a mistake. . . .*

Twilight nuzzled her hair. "Look, we can sort this out later. We should be trying to find Jo-Ann now."

His words jerked Lauren back to reality. "You're right!" she exclaimed. Jo-Ann needed their help. "We need a seeing stone."

Taking hold of his mane, she swung herself on to his back.

"Over by the tree!" Twilight said, and he cantered toward the edge of the field. He halted under the large oak tree beside a pinkish-gray rock of rose quartz. Twilight bent his head and touched the rock with his horn. "Help us find Jo-Ann," he murmured.

There was a burst of purple smoke and the surface of the rock turned into a shimmering mirror. In the mirror, a picture formed of a girl lying in a crumpled heap on a frosty track.

"It's Jo-Ann!" Lauren gasped. "She's injured! And she must be freezing!" She looked closer at the picture. "It's the clearing with the banks!" she said. "Come on, let's fly there!"

Twilight nodded eagerly. Lauren climbed onto his back and, with a snort, he plunged into the sky.

The wind whipped against Lauren's cheeks as they swooped through the air. She'd been desperate to fly again ever since Twilight told her he was losing his powers, but now she was too worried to enjoy it. Her heart thudded wildly. How badly injured was Jo-Ann? She had been lying so still in the seeing stone. Fear gripped Lauren. "Faster, Twilight!"

He tossed his head and galloped faster over the trees.

Although the clearing was quite hard to get to by following the tracks in the woods, Twilight got there in no time at all, flying above the treetops. "There she is!" he cried as they swooped into the clearing.

Jo-Ann was lying at the bottom of the steepest bank, beside a jump made out of branches and logs. Her eyes were closed and her leg was twisted at a strange angle.

"She must have tried that jump!" Lauren gasped.

Twilight landed beside Jo-Ann and Lauren scrambled off his back.

"She's still breathing," Twilight said in relief.

"Jo-Ann?" Lauren said gently.

The girl didn't move.

Lauren turned to Twilight. "What do we do?"

"I'll try and help her with my magic." Twilight bent down until his horn was touching Jo-Ann's leg. Lauren watched as he closed his eyes in concentration. They had used his magic powers before to heal wounds but no one had ever needed it as much as Jo-Ann did now.

Please let this work, Lauren prayed. *Please let Twilight's magic help Jo-Ann.*

CHAPTER

Nine

Twilight's horn shone even brighter. For a moment nothing happened, but then Lauren saw some of the tension leave Jo-Ann's face, and she shifted so that her leg was lying more naturally. Twilight lightly touched his horn against Jo-Ann's forehead. Again it glowed with magic. A few seconds later, Jo-Ann's eyelids fluttered and she sighed.

"The magic needs some time to work," Twilight whispered to Lauren. "Her leg was broken and she had a bad bump on her head, but I think she'll be OK."

Lauren's knees felt weak with relief. "We should get her home. Will it be all right to move her?" She knew it could be dangerous to move someone who was badly injured.

Twilight nodded. "My magic will protect her."

"Let's take her to the Cassidys' farm," Lauren suggested. "It's closer, and that's where the search party was meeting."

Twilight nodded and knelt down so that Lauren could lift Jo-Ann onto his back. She was bigger than Lauren, and because she was

unconscious it was hard to get her onto Twilight's back, but at last Lauren managed it. Scrambling up beside her, she put her arms around her and Twilight smoothly took off.

As they flew, color started to return to Jo-Ann's cheeks. Lauren held on to her tightly. *Please let Twilight be right,* she thought, *please let her be OK.*

Suddenly Twilight tensed. "There are some people ahead. I can hear their voices. I'd better fly around another way. We don't want them to see us."

Lauren started to nod, but then she had a thought. "It could be part of the search party looking for Jo-Ann. I bet they've come to check the clearing." She strained her ears but couldn't hear anything. "Can you tell who it is, Twilight?"

Hovering in the air, Twilight listened hard. "I can hear your dad and a few other people. I think one of them's Mrs. Cassidy!"

Lauren felt a rush of relief. "Let's fly down. If I turn you into a pony I can say I rode to the clearing and found Jo-Ann there."

Twilight nodded and cantered down. As he landed behind some oak trees, Jo-Ann stirred and her eyelids fluttered. Lauren had a feeling that she was turning Twilight back into a pony just in time!

She helped Jo-Ann off Twilight's back and gently leaned her against the trunk of a tree.

"Where am I?" Jo-Ann murmured, still with her eyes closed.

Lauren quickly whispered the words of the Undoing Spell.

There was a purple flash and Jo-Ann's eyes shot open. "What was that?" she gasped.

"Nothing," Lauren said as Twilight transformed into a pony behind Jo-Ann.

Jo-Ann blinked and stared at her. "Lauren? Is that you? Where am I?"

"In the woods," Lauren replied. "I think you must have fallen off Beauty and been knocked out. Don't worry, there are people coming. They'll be able to help."

Twilight whinnied loudly, and through the trees Lauren heard the sound of voices getting closer. "We're over here!" she called.

As Twilight whinnied again, Jo-Ann gripped Lauren's arms. "Where's Beauty? Is she OK?"

"She's at home," Lauren said. "She's fine. She went back to the stables without you."

Jo-Ann rubbed her eyes. "I can't remember anything. I was riding Beauty and then . . ." She hesitated. "I can remember this weird feeling, like I was flying on a horse through the air."

Lauren hid a smile. "You must have bumped your head pretty hard!"

Jo-Ann laughed weakly. "Yeah, flying! As if!"

Just then, the search party arrived. Lauren's dad was with Mrs. Cassidy and a few other adults that Lauren didn't know. They looked very relieved to see Jo-Ann sitting up and talking.

One of them, a woman with short blonde hair, ran forward. "Jo, honey! Are you OK?"

"I'm fine, Mom," said Jo-Ann. "I've just got a terrible headache and my leg hurts a bit. The last thing I remember is being on Beauty. I guess I must have tried to ride too fast down the slope and fallen off. It was a really dumb thing to do. I'm sorry."

Her mom hugged her hard. "The most important thing is that you're OK. It's lucky you weren't badly hurt!"

"I'll call my husband," said Mrs. Cassidy,

taking her phone out of her pocket. "He'll bring the pickup to take Jo-Ann home. Then we should let the others know we've found her."

Mr. Foster hurried over to Lauren. "What were you doing in the woods? How did you find Jo-Ann?"

Lauren took a breath. "Well, after you and Mom had gone, I realized that Jo-Ann might be in the clearing where we've been riding. So I got Twilight and decided to have a look." *It's almost the truth,* she thought. "I found her lying by the slope," she went on. "I put her on Twilight and started to bring her home. Then I heard your voices, so we shouted to you."

Her dad hugged her. "Well done. Though, really, you shouldn't have gone out into the woods on your own in the dark. It would have been best to call us first."

"I'm sorry," Lauren said.

"It's OK." Her dad smiled. "It all worked out fine in the end."

There was the sound of an engine and headlights appeared through the trees. Jo-Ann's mom and Mrs. Cassidy helped Jo-Ann up. "Time to get you home," said Mrs. Cassidy.

Jo-Ann turned to look at Lauren. "Thanks for finding me, Lauren."

Lauren smiled. "That's OK. See you."

"Yeah." Jo-Ann smiled back as her mom helped her toward the truck. She was limping, but her leg wasn't broken like it had been in the clearing. Twilight's magic had worked!

Mr. Foster put an arm around Lauren's shoulders. "Do you want me to walk back with you?"

"It's OK," she said. "You go in the truck. I'll ride Twilight. It's not far and I'll probably get home faster."

Her dad nodded. "OK. I know you'll be safe with Twilight." He patted Twilight's neck. "Best pony in the world, aren't you, fella?"

Twilight snorted.

"See you at home." Mr. Foster smiled.

He hurried to join the others in the truck. As the sound of the engine faded, Lauren turned to Twilight. Now that all the excitement was over, she realized that they had some talking to do. She said the words of the Turning Spell.

In a second, Twilight was a unicorn again.

For a moment neither of them spoke. When they'd been helping Jo-Ann, everything else had been forgotten — all the unhappiness, all the lies, all the worries about what would happen next. But now that they were alone again, everything came flooding back.

Lauren cleared her throat. "So, you're not going back to Arcadia?"

"No." Twilight took a breath. "No, I'm not."

Their eyes met and they both took a step toward each other, speaking at the same time.

"Oh, Twilight, I felt so —"

"I'm sorry, Lauren, I never meant —"

They both stopped.

"You go first," Twilight said.

"No, you," Lauren told him.

He lifted his muzzle to her face. "I'm sorry," he breathed. "I never meant to hurt you. I only lied about my powers going because I thought it would make things easier for you. I love you, Lauren."

She swallowed. "I know. I love you, too. But I wish you'd told me the truth all along. When I saw you with that other unicorn in the sky, I thought that you'd been lying because you were planning on going back to Arcadia without telling me. It was awful, the worst feeling ever." She touched his neck. "It's kind of my fault though. I should have known better. I should have trusted you."

"I should have told you the truth."

Twilight sighed. "I just felt so confused.
It's a great honor to be asked to go back
to Arcadia. I've never heard of a unicorn
saying no."

Lauren looked at him. "But you did."

Twilight nodded. "For you."

Lauren rested her forehead against his. She was remembering what he had told her before. "Is it true that if you don't go, you'll lose your magic powers?"

Twilight nodded. "That's what the Elder said. But I don't care. So long as I'm with you, Lauren, I don't mind giving up my magic."

Lauren bit her lip. She knew how much his magic meant to him. *I can't make him give it up for me,* she thought. *I can't.* No matter how much it hurt, she had to let him go. "You . . ." Her voice dropped to a whisper. "You should go."

Twilight took a step back. "What?"

Lauren's heart felt like it was breaking. But she couldn't make him give up his magic.

"Twilight, you have to go back," she said, tears filling her eyes. "You're brilliant at using your powers. Look how you helped Jo-Ann tonight. If you were in Arcadia you could help so many people. I can't keep you here."

"But I don't want to leave you, Lauren," Twilight said desperately.

"You have to." A sob burst from her. "We both know you do."

"No," Twilight said, shaking his head in dismay.

Just then, there was the sound of a twig snapping behind them. They swung around in alarm.

A Unicorn Elder was standing in the trees at the side of the clearing. She was much bigger than Twilight, and her silver horn glittered in the moonlight.

Lauren stared at the unicorn in horror, a single thought leaping into her head.

She's come to take Twilight away.

CHAPTER

Ten

The Unicorn Elder stepped forward and bowed her head. "Hello, Lauren."

Lauren couldn't speak. She gripped Twilight's mane.

"My name is Sidra," said the unicorn.

Twilight faced the unicorn bravely. "I won't go! I won't! I told you —"

"It's all right, Twilight," Sidra interrupted

him. "I have not come to take you away." Her beautiful eyes shone. "Quite the opposite, in fact."

Twilight stared at her, puzzled.

"What do you mean?" Lauren asked.

Sidra looked from Lauren to Twilight. "I, and some of the other Elders, have been watching tonight as you helped the injured girl. It made us realize that although the mirror has chosen Twilight to come back to Arcadia and train as an Elder's assistant, now is not the time. So, Twilight, we have decided that you can stay. It is clear you can do a lot of good with Lauren. As much, maybe even more, than you could do with us in Arcadia."

"I can stay!" Twilight breathed.

"Will he still have his magic powers?" Lauren wondered.

Sidra nodded.

"Oh, Twilight!" Lauren gasped, throwing her arms around his neck.

Sidra smiled. "You love each other and deserve to be together. The Unicorn Elders are sure you will do many good things."

"Oh, we will!" Lauren promised. "At least we'll try to, won't we, Twilight?"

"Definitely!" he said. "Thank you! Thank you so much!"

The unicorn bowed her head again. "We thank you for all the good deeds you have already done, and wish you good luck for the future." She touched her magnificent silver horn to Twilight's forehead and then to Lauren's. Lauren felt a tingly warm feeling spread through her.

Magic! she thought.

The unicorn blinked warmly at her. "You are a very special unicorn friend, Lauren. Very special indeed."

Lauren felt overwhelmed with pride and happiness.

"And now I must go," Sidra said, tossing back her mane. "Come, you may fly beside me some of the way if you wish."

"Yes, please!" Lauren said, and Twilight nodded eagerly.

Lauren climbed on to his back and twisted her fingers in his silky mane as he and the Elder plunged into the sky. The

stars whizzed past in a glittering stream and the wind whipped Lauren's hair back from her face. She didn't think she had ever flown so fast or so high! She laughed out loud as Twilight tossed his head in delight and galloped even faster beside the snow-white

Unicorn Elder with the glittering silver horn.

"I must leave you here!" Sidra said, halting and rearing up against the dark sky. "Good-bye, Lauren! Good-bye, Twilight! Good luck!"

"Good-bye!" they called.

And with a flash of purple light, Sidra disappeared.

"Oh, wow!" Lauren gasped. "Wasn't that fun!"

"The best!" Twilight agreed.

"I guess we should go home now," Lauren sighed. "Dad will be wondering where I am."

Circling in the sky, they flew back toward Granger's Farm. They landed at the edge of the woods so Lauren could turn Twilight back to a pony in case her mom and dad were looking out for them.

Just before saying the words of the spell, she pressed her cheek against his neck. There was one more thing she wanted to clear up. "You know that time I overheard you saying, 'I have to tell her'? You really didn't mean me, did you?"

"No," Twilight said. "I was thinking about Sidra. I knew I had to tell her that I couldn't leave you." He turned and blew gently in her hair. "I'm sorry you ever thought I would."

"I'm sorry too," Lauren said. "I should have trusted you more."

"And I should have trusted you," Twilight replied. "If I had told you the truth from the start, you wouldn't have been so upset."

"I probably would have," Lauren admitted, thinking honestly about how she would have reacted if he'd told her he'd been asked to go back to Arcadia. "But at least we could have talked it through together. Like best friends." She stroked his nose. "So from now on, no more secrets. Promise?"

"No more secrets," Twilight agreed.

Lauren smiled and said the words of the Undoing Spell.

In a flash, Twilight was a pony again. Looking at him standing there, with his fluffy gray coat and pricked-up ears, Lauren felt a rush of love. He was her pony, her unicorn, but most of all he was her best friend.

Putting an arm around his neck, she kissed him. "Come on," she said happily. "Let's go home."

My Secret Unicorn

Twilight Magic

"Goodness," said Mrs. Wakefield. "You should

feel very honored, Lauren. Apart from me,

you're the only person Apple has

approached since Currant's been born. You

must have a real way with horses."

Lauren felt a glow of pride. Jessica and Mel

grinned at her but Jade looked cross that

Lauren was getting all the attention . . .